P9-DXD-498

With love,
from Nancy
to

the moms—
Alexine and Berta

Sarah, Bob,
Ana and Sophia

Nancy, Tom,
Olivia and Colton

Linda, David, Matthew,
Maya
and Michael

Donna, Jeff,
Jordan and Lindsay

Joe, Anna
and Gina

Dee, Joe
and Mia

Ginny, Tom
and Sky

Wyatt, Lisa
and Marlon

Amy, Eric,
Momie and Tyler

Margery, Anahid,
Deirdre, Virginia, and
Adam

Doe, Judy,
Kay, Leslie B.,
Leslie C.

Lorraine,
Mary-Kelly,
Nancy A.

Bina, Kate D.,
Kate F., Lynn,
Pat, Barbara

**and always
for
Peter**

On February 14th, Mrs. Bloom asked, "Who is our calendar helper today?"

Marshall Cavendish, 99 White Plains Road, Tarrytown, NY 10591
www.marshallcavendish.com
Library of Congress Cataloging-in-Publication Data

Wallace, Nancy Elizabeth.
The Valentine Express / written and illustrated by Nancy Elizabeth Wallace.—1st ed.
p. cm.
Summary: Minna and Pip make Valentine's Day gifts for their neighbors after learning about the history of the holiday at school.
ISBN 0-7614-5183-8
[1. Valentine's Day—Fiction. 2. Schools—Fiction. 3. Rabbits—Fiction.] I. Title.

PZ7.W15875Val 2004
[E]—dc22
2004000914

The text of this book is set in Goudy.
The illustrations are rendered in cut paper.
Book design by Virginia Pope

Printed in China
First edition
1 3 5 6 4 2

The Valentine Express

Written and Illustrated by
Nancy Elizabeth Wallace

Marshall Cavendish
New York ♥ London ♥ Singapore

"Me!" said Minna. "It's Valentine's Day!"

She taped a paper heart over the 14.

"Let's talk about Valentine's Day," said Mrs. Bloom. "Would anyone like to share?"

“Valentine’s Day is about love and friendship,” said Minna.

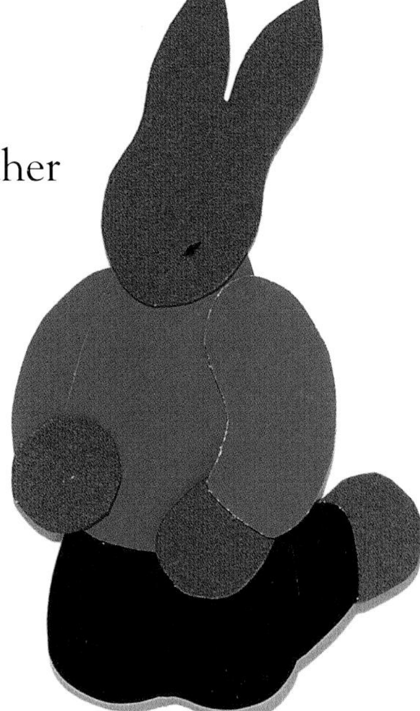

“And giving each other cards,” added Tyrone.

“And candy,” said Lindsey.

“My dad gave my mom flowers,” said Vanessa.

“It’s about saying and doing nice things,” said Miguel. “And everybody being everybody’s friend.”

“Yes, it’s a day to be extra thoughtful and caring,” agreed Mrs. Bloom.

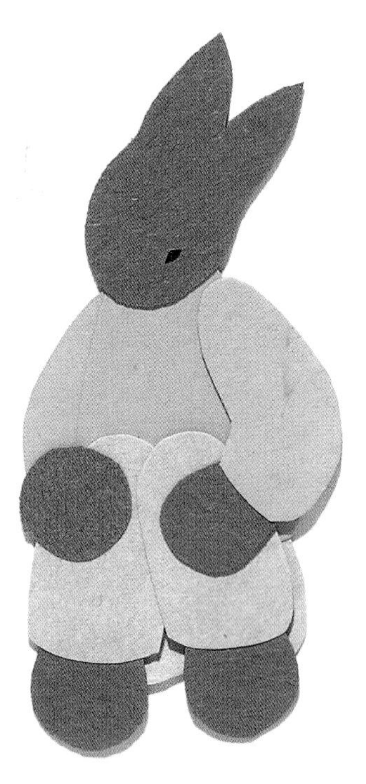

"But how did celebrating Valentine's Day begin?" she asked. "Nobody really knows! It may have started in ancient Rome. During a festival held in February, young men picked names from an urn in hopes of finding someone to marry.

"It may have started with someone named Valentine who lived long, long ago. There are several stories about Valentine. One story tells how he was kind to children and that he sent a note to a young friend and signed it 'from your Valentine.'

"Or it may have started because in the old days everyone thought the birds found their mates on February 14th."

"It may have started for all these reasons. But one thing we do know for sure—for hundreds of years, sweethearts have been sending each other notes and cards, gifts and flowers."

Mrs. Bloom pointed to her heart.

"The heart and feelings go together. We say things like, 'You're my sweetheart, my heart throbs for you.' So what shape is a symbol of love?"

The class knew. "The heart," they shouted.

"And I'm sure you know who this is!" said Mrs. Bloom.

The class shouted, "Cupid!"

"Oh no, not more love stuff," groaned Dave.

Mrs. Bloom smiled. "Long, long ago people also believed there really was a Cupid. If he shot a magic golden arrow into someone's heart, that person would fall in love."

"Today, Valentine's Day is celebrated in many countries around the world."

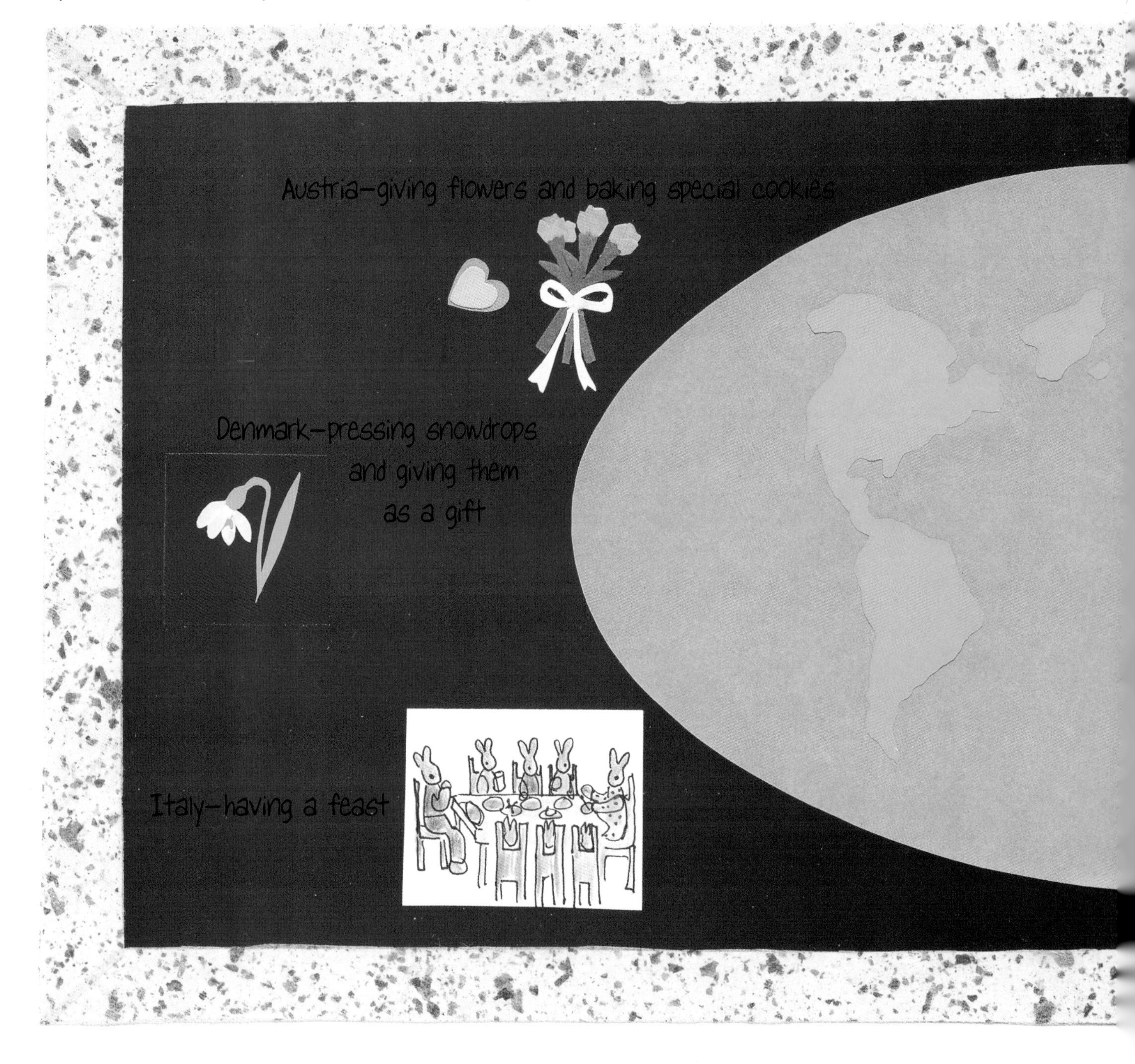

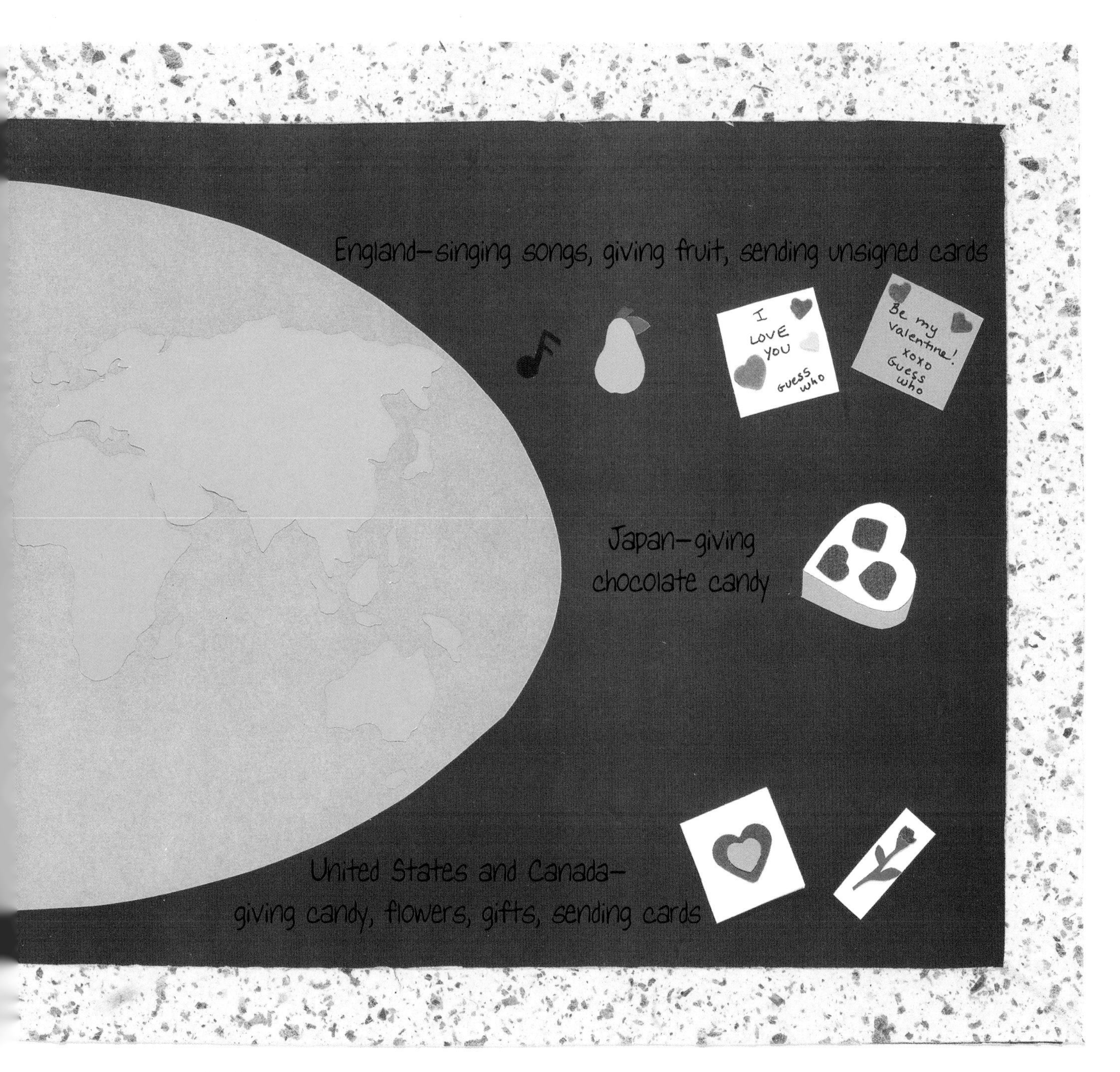

Knock, knock, knock. Someone was at the classroom door.

"Come in," called Mrs. Bloom.

Vanessa's mom brought in two plates of heart-shaped cookies.

Minna's dad brought in a pitcher of pink-lemonade punch.

And everyone gave everyone valentines.

My
4 U
Happy Valentine's Day
to a
great teacher
Do not open
until Valentine's Day
my
Valentine
XOXOXOXO
SWAK

After school Minna and Pip walked home. When they got to their street, Mrs. Wunder was hobbling toward them.

"Happy Valentine's Day, Mrs. Wunder!" they said.

"Oh, is it today? Looks like your bags are filled with valentines."

Minna answered, "I got one from every bunny in my class!"

"I got one from every bunny in my class, too," said Pip. "Did you get lots, Mrs. Wunder?"

"I used to when I was young," she said. "Well, happy Valentine's Day."

She went into her house. Minna and Pip kept walking.

"I wonder if grown-ups get valentines," said Minna. "What if Mrs. Wunder didn't get any? I wonder if Madame Dodie got one or Mr. and Mrs. Checker."

"Or Big Stewart!" they said together.

"Let's make valentines for them!" said Minna.

When they got home, they told Dad about their idea.

"That's a very thoughtful thing to do," he said. "While you're creating valentines, I'll be in the kitchen cooking something special for supper and dessert! Don't peek!"

"We won't!"

Minna went and got her art box. It was filled with colored paper, a glue stick and markers, scissors and string, wooden craft sticks, tape, and a pencil.

Pip got his scissors.

"Can you make a valentine, Pip?" asked Minna.

"Hearts are hard to cut, Minna."

"Just do your best."

Pip started cutting. Minna did, too.

She cut out one big paper heart and wrote on it. Then she cut it into puzzle pieces.

Be my

Valen tine

"A puzzle for Mrs. Wunder," said Minna.

She put all of the puzzle pieces into a white envelope.

“Oo-la-la,” said Minna. “I have a great idea for Madame Dodie!”

She cut a large triangle. Then she cut two hearts for wings and cut a blue butterfly body. She pasted the butterfly onto the triangle.

Pip held the triangle while Minna taped it to a skinny stick.

“*Voilá*! A flag for Madame Dodie!” said Minna.

"Mr. and Mrs. Checker *love* playing games. Instead of tic-tac-toe," said Minna, giggling, "I will make them tic-tac-heart."

Minna took a piece of pink paper and a piece of purple paper. She folded the pink paper in half and then in half again. She cut out four pink hearts, then four more pink hearts. She did the same thing with the purple paper.

Next, she measured a square and cut it.

Then, she took some more purple and pink paper and cut out four skinny strips to fit the square.

Pip helped hold the paper strips straight while Minna glued them in place.

"Mr. and Mrs. Checker are going to love playing this game," said Minna. She put five pink hearts and five purple hearts and the square into a big envelope.

"Now," said Minna. "Time to deliver. Puzzle for Mrs. Wunder, flag for Madame Dodie, tic-tac-toe—I mean heart—for Mr. and Mrs. Checker, and for Big Stewart . . ."

Pip held something in his hands behind his back. "These are not good hearts, Minna."

"Can I see?" Minna asked.

Pip put some of his hearts on the table and stuffed the rest into his pocket. "They are my practice hearts."

Minna thought for a minute. "That's OK, Pip. You were busy helping me."

"Do you have an idea, Minna?" he asked.

"I'm thinking," she said.

"You have extra hearts, Minna," said Pip.

"We can make . . . We can make a—"

“Mobile!” she shouted.

Minna got two craft sticks and string from her art box. Holding the sticks in an X, she wound string around and around the middle. Next, she cut four pieces of string the same length. She and Pip taped two purple hearts and two pink hearts to the strings.

Then, Minna tied the strings to the ends of the sticks.

Now they had a mobile for Big Stewart.

"We better carry this valentine," said Minna. "So it doesn't get all tangled."

They loaded Pip's wagon.

"We're the Valentine Express," said Minna, "delivering valentines to Mrs. Wunder and Madame Dodie and Mr. and Mrs. Checker and Big Stewart."

"Have fun!" said Dad. "But hurry along, it's getting close to supper time."

“Happy Valentine’s Day, Mrs. Wunder! A heart-shaped puzzle for you!”

“Oh! How clever! How nice! Thank you, Minna and Pip.”

At the next house Pip buzzed the buzzer. Madame Dodie opened the door, and he handed her the flag. "Happy Valentine's Day!"

"Happy Valentine's Day to you, *mes amis*." Madame Dodie waved her flag.

"*Merci beaucoup!*"

Minna clanged the bell at the third house.

"Well, look who's here," said Mr. Checker.

Minna said, "Valentine Express, delivering a game for you."

"And a pretty mobile for the Mrs.!" said Mr. Checker.

"Ooooooh," said Mrs. Checker. "I will hang it in the kitchen. You are filling our home with hearts and love. Thank you, sweet neighbors!"

"But," started Pip.

Minna grabbed Pip's hand. "*But* we'd better be going."

At the end of the Checkers' path, the Valentine Express stopped.

Minna sighed. "Mrs. Checker loved our mobile! But now we don't have a valentine for Big Stewart."

"What will we do, Minna?" asked Pip.

"I'm thinking," said Minna.

"Do you have an idea, Minna?" Pip asked.

"I'm still thinking," she answered.

Then she said, "If only we had your hearts, Pip."

"They are in my pocket, Minna," he said.

"They are? Good!" she said. "Now we need to find a big twig."

Pip found one near a tree. He brought it over to Minna.

Minna gently pushed Pip's hearts onto the small branches.

"Wow!" said Pip. "I like it."

The Valentine Express was making deliveries again.

Ding, ding, dooong.

"What do we have here?" asked Big Stewart. "Come in, Minna and Pip! What a creative valentine!"

Big Stewart put his valentine in a vase on the mantel.
"It's perfect," he said. "It's the art of friendship."

Then Minna and Pip and the Valentine Express headed home.